The Case of the Stolen Bagels

STORY BY **Hila Colman**

PICTURES BY **Pat Grant Porter**

Crown Publishers, Inc.
New York

Text copyright©1977 by Hila Colman
Illustrations copyright©1977 by Pat Grant Porter
All rights reserved. No part of this publication may be reproduced, stored in a retrieval system,
or transmitted, in any form or by any means, electronic, mechanical, photocopying, recording,
or otherwise, without prior written permission of the publisher. Inquiries should be addressed to
Crown Publishers, Inc., One Park Avenue, New York, N.Y. 10016. Manufactured in the United
States of America. Published simultaneously in Canada by General Publishing Company Limited.

10   9   8   7   6   5   4   3   2   1

The text of this book is set in 14 pt. Times Roman.
The illustrations are black-and-white halftone.

Library of Congress Cataloging in Publication Data

Colman, Hila. The case of the stolen bagels.
SUMMARY: When Paul is wrongly accused of stealing bagels intended for an art project in his
classroom, he sets out to find the real culprit. [1. School stories. 2. Mystery and detective stories]
I. Porter, Patricia Grant. II. Title. PZ7.C7Cas   [Fic]   77-10029   ISBN 0-517-53064-3

Also by Hila Colman

Nobody Has to Be a Kid Forever
Ethan's Favorite Teacher
Diary of a Frantic Kid Sister

Paul sat eating his breakfast and looking out of the window. He didn't like what he saw: his school and the playground. He wished that his house was miles away so that he wouldn't have to look at that place every day of his life.

The only good thing about that particular morning was what he was eating. Freshly toasted, crunchy, chewy bagels. Paul loved bagels. Sometimes he had them with cream cheese and sometimes he had them with just butter, and sometimes he grabbed one from the bag and ate it plain. "A real bagel lover," his mother called him.

Paul munched his second bagel as slowly as possible. When he was finished he'd have to walk across his lawn and go to school.

"I wish I could eat as many bagels as you do and not get fat," his mother said to him. She was an attractive woman who ate cottage cheese and cucumbers to stay slim. "One of these days you're going to turn into a bagel."

"I wish I would," said Paul.

"Would you like to go around with a hole in your middle?" joked his mother.

"At least I wouldn't have to go to school." Paul was trying to decide whether to eat a third bagel. He compromised by slicing one in half.

"I thought you liked school," said his mother.

"I changed my mind. I don't like it any more."

"You're just in a bad mood. You'll get over it. You had better go or you'll be late. Have a good day."

Paul turned around and made a face. "Fat chance."

Paul hadn't always hated school. But something had happened on Friday that had made him change his mind. Something he had not told his parents about. They had been busy over the weekend and there hadn't been time. He knew he really hadn't wanted to talk about it anyway. He didn't even want to think about it. But now it was Monday, and Monday meant school.

The truth was, Paul had gotten into TROUBLE. (That's the way he thought about it, in big capital letters.) And all because of that twerp, Dick Matthews. He wished Dick Matthews would just disappear. Dick had already gotten him into trouble once before. A week or so ago, Dick grabbed his sweater and went running around the playground with it. Naturally Paul ran after him, and when he grabbed hold of Dick, he whacked him on the back with a stick. It wasn't a hard whack, but Dick cried like a baby and went running to their teacher, Mrs. Dennis.

Mrs. Dennis sat Paul down and gave him one of her talks. "That temper of yours is going to get you into real trouble one of these days," she said.

That wasn't the first time Paul had been warned about his temper. His parents told him that it worried them too and he had been trying to be careful. Things had been going pretty well for him until Friday. As far as he was concerned he had been minding his own business making his clay pot. He was very proud when he took it out of the kiln; he was going to put it in the art show.

Then Dick Matthews ran into him and knocked the pot out of his hands. It fell to the floor and broke into a hundred pieces.

"You dumb jerk," Paul had screamed. "You did it on purpose. I'll break your neck . . ."

"I'm sorry, Paul. I didn't mean it," Dick had said.

"You saw me standing here, you ran right into me. Don't tell me you didn't do it on purpose, I know you did." Paul was furious and without thinking he punched Dick in the stomach. Dick fell against a table holding a couple of tall jars and paintbrushes and a pile of posters the students had made. The jars spilled over and the colored water ran all over the posters, ruining them.

Mrs. Dennis, who had stepped out of the room for a few minutes, hurried back when she heard the noise. "What's going on here?" she had demanded.

"He punched me in the stomach," shouted Dick.

"He broke my pot," yelled Paul.

"That was an accident," said Dick. "I told him I was sorry."

"Did you punch Dick?" asked Mrs. Dennis.

"Yes I did," said Paul. "But I had a good reason." Paul was both frightened and angry.

"There is never a good reason for punching anyone, Paul. Dick said it was an accident and he was sorry. That was enough. All the posters are ruined."

"I didn't mean to ruin the posters," said Paul. "But Dick broke my pot."

"I'm sorry about your pot. But that's still no excuse for

punching Dick. I think you had better go see Mr. Hartman."

In the principal's office, Mr. Hartman said, "You seem to be getting into a lot of trouble lately. Is anything bothering you?"

"Nothing is bothering me," said Paul. "I just don't like it when someone does something mean to me."

"Why do you always think someone is being mean? Do you think you're mean if you bump into another kid accidentally?" Mr. Hartman asked.

"Not if it's an accident," Paul said. "But that wasn't. He was looking right at me."

"Maybe you thought he saw you, or maybe Dick's mind was somewhere else. You don't give anyone the benefit of the doubt. Hitting is no solution, anyway."

"Yes sir," Paul said. But he was sure that it was not an

accident. Mr. Hartman gave him a pat on the shoulder when he left and said, "Take it easy."

As he headed toward school, Paul tried not to think about what had happened on Friday. He was determined to turn over a new leaf. When he reached his classroom, he stood still and sniffed. He couldn't believe it. It was impossible. But Paul knew that smell anywhere. Sitting on the floor next to his teacher's desk were two huge brown paper bags of fresh bagels. Paul couldn't resist. He picked up a bagel and bit into it.

"Paul Brody, you put that bagel right down." Mrs. Dennis's voice made him jump.

He was halfway into another bite. "Paul, you heard me. Put that right down."

Paul chewed and swallowed as fast as he could. "I started it, Mrs. Dennis."

"I don't care. Throw the rest into the wastebasket."

"Can't I finish it?"

"No, you cannot. These bagels are here for a purpose. They are not to be eaten."

Paul looked at her wide-eyed. "What else do you do with bagels?"

"We're going to paint them," said Mrs. Dennis cheerfully.

"Paint them!" said Paul. "You don't paint bagels, Mrs. Dennis, you eat them."

"I know all about bagels," said Mrs. Dennis. "We have them every Sunday for breakfast. But we're going to make Christmas decorations with these bagels."

"Christmas decorations!" said Paul.

"You heard me. Now go to your seat, and keep your hands off the bagels."

"It's the smell," said Paul, sniffing the air. "I mean if they didn't smell so terrific . . ."

"Just stop smelling."

"You mean I should stop breathing?" asked Paul.

Mrs. Dennis smiled. "That'll keep your mind off the bagels. See how long you can hold your breath."

"Thanks a lot," said Paul.

But all morning long the only thing Paul could think about

was the bagels. He became more and more annoyed at the idea of painting them. Mrs. Dennis's explanation only made it worse. "This afternoon we're going to spread the bagels out to dry overnight. They have to be hard and dry before we paint them. Tomorrow, or the next day, when they're good and dry we can paint them. We have a wide assortment of acrylic paints, and if you do a good job we can sell them in the art show for Christmas decorations. That will give us money for our spring trip. I think it will be fun."

"Couldn't we have a bagel-eating contest instead?" asked Paul. "I bet I could eat a whole bagful."

"I bet you could, Paul, but that's not what we're going to do."

In the afternoon Mrs. Dennis asked two of the children to help her clear off some tables in the art room. The minute they were out of the room, Dick Matthews dared Paul to take a bagel.

Paul looked Dick straight in the eye. "I don't want one," he said.

"You're just chicken," said Dick.

Paul stood undecided.

"Paul is a chicken. Paul is a chicken," sang Dick.

"Get lost," said Paul. He went past Dick to the front of the room and stood next to the bags of bagels. He didn't even have his hand on one when Mrs. Dennis walked into the room.

"Paul Brody, *what are you doing?*"

"Nothing," said Paul.

"You were about to take a bagel. Don't tell me you weren't."

"I was just looking at them."

"Go back to your seat," said Mrs. Dennis.

Paul didn't even look at Dick as he walked past him and went to his desk.

And the day wasn't over for him yet. When the class went into the art room for their art class, Mrs. Dennis said that she thought it was a good day to make new posters to replace those that had been spoiled.

"Paul should make them. He's the one who spoiled them," said Betty Haines.

"That seems fair," said Mrs. Dennis. "Paul, you make new posters and the rest of you can work with the clay."

"I hate making posters," said Paul. "I want to make another pot for the art show."

"You can make a new pot another time."

"It's not fair," Paul mumbled. Mrs. Dennis paid no attention.

Paul sat doing nothing until Mrs. Dennis told him to hurry up and get to work. He took as long as he could getting the poster paper and the paints.

He looked at the bagels spread out on a table to dry. He wished he could take all the bagels and throw them at Dick Matthews. Or maybe at Mrs. Dennis.

Paul hadn't even finished one poster when the bell rang. Mrs. Dennis was annoyed. "You'd better get with it, Paul. Tomorrow when we're having fun painting the bagels you're going to be doing more posters."

"Maybe the bagels will rot overnight," said Paul glumly.

"They'd better not," said Mrs. Dennis.

Paul was pretty unhappy when he came home from school that day. His mother asked, "What's the matter?"

"Nothing," Paul told her.

His mother's face showed that she didn't believe him. "You don't have to tell me about it if you don't want to. But maybe I can help."

Paul shook his head. "Forget it."

Paul sat up in his room and moped. He couldn't even get excited about his rock collection. Paul's minerals and rocks and stones were his most precious possessions. Some he had picked up from his own brook and some from old dirt roads. Others he had found on vacation trips with his parents. He had striped stones from Lake Champlain, colored stones from beaches on Cape Cod and Maine. He had stones he had collected from beaches in Florida.

Paul was still moping when his mother announced that his friend George had arrived.

George came thumping up the stairs to Paul's room.

"What do you want to do?" asked George.

"I dunno."

"Let's go out," said George.

Paul agreed.

First they went down to the stream that ran alongside Paul's house. It was fun stepping from rock to rock, and Paul couldn't resist picking up small stones for his collection. Soon his pockets were bulging.

When they got tired of walking the brook, they turned up a dirt road to Garnet Road. This was Paul's favorite place: an old wagon road that a long time ago had been paved with rough garnets. They walked slowly, their heads down and their eyes searching for garnets.

"I got a beaut," George called out. He showed Paul a big stone cut into an almost perfect octagonal shape.

"Boy, look at this one." Paul picked up one that was even bigger.

Paul and George vied with each other to see who could gather more garnets. By the time they were ready to go home they both had as much as they could put into their pockets.

Paul had to throw away some of the stones he had picked up in the brook.

Back at Paul's house, they washed the stones until they were clean. Paul lined his garnets up on a shelf with his others and George put his into a bag to take home. Then Paul put his other stones into his tumbler to get smoothed and ready for polishing. The tumbler had been a Christmas present the year before, and Paul liked it. It had three little rubber baskets that turned when he plugged the cord into an electric socket in his wall. The first basket had a coarse abrasive in it, the next one a medium one, and the last one a fine one for pre-polishing. The stones got tumbled in each basket, beginning with the coarse abrasive. Paul often let the tumbler run all night, and he liked to listen to it before he fell asleep.

They put Paul's new stones into the tumbler and started it. "You have a great collection," said George. "What are you going to do with it?"

"Nothing. Just keep it."

"You could put it in the art show. I bet we could sell some of those stones and make a lot of money for our class trip."

"I wouldn't put my collection in the art show. It stinks."

Paul had almost forgotten his troubles and he wished that George hadn't reminded him.

"Painting bagels is kind of dumb," said George.

"It's stupid. I wish they'd all disappear. I'd like to eat them all," Paul said. "I bet I could eat a hundred."

George laughed. He puffed out his cheeks into a fat face. "You'd blow up like a balloon and explode."

Paul bounced out of bed the next morning the way he usually did. Soon after he was up, however, he remembered that he was going to have to make more posters while his classmates painted. He decided that the best way out was not to go to school.

"Mom," he said, "I have a stomachache."

His mother put her hand on his forehead. "You don't have any fever, and you look healthy enough." She studied his face. "I think you don't want to go to school. I knew yesterday something was bothering you. Today I'm certain."

"My stomach really hurts," Paul said.

"You'd better go to school, and if you don't feel well later, you can always come home. All you have to do is walk across the lawn. That's one good thing about living next to the school."

"I wish school was a million miles away," Paul said.

Paul walked into his classroom just as the bell was ringing. But no one was there. Paul could hear noise coming from the art room. He thought he would sit at his desk and not go in there.

But his curiosity got the better of him. He could tell from

the noise that something was going on in there.

"There he is, there he is." The children were shouting and pointing at Paul when he appeared in the art room.

Mrs. Dennis turned around. "Paul Brody," she said, "I cannot believe you would do anything like this." She threw up her hands in despair. "I don't know what to say. It's a wonder you're not sick."

"I am sick," said Paul. He did feel sick, now that he saw what they were all excited about. A lot of the bagels were gone, and some were half-eaten and on the floor. There were crumbs all over the place. "I didn't do it," he said.

Mrs. Dennis just kept looking at him. Paul had never seen her quite this way. She looked as if she were almost ready to cry. "I don't know what to say, Paul. It's hard to believe anyone would deliberately do such a thing."

"But I didn't do it, Mrs. Dennis." Paul could feel his anger rising, but this time it was mingled with fear. "I swear I didn't."

"You'd better go see Mr. Hartman." Mrs. Dennis looked down at the broken bagels, and Paul thought he saw tears in her eyes.

Paul sat nervously in Mr. Hartman's office. The principal knew all about what had happened. "What on earth made you do such a thing, Paul?"

Paul shook his head. "I didn't do it," he said.

"I'd like to believe you," Mr. Hartman said. "But everyone heard you carrying on about the bagels, and you were angry about lettering the posters. The fact that you live next door to the school would make it easy for you to slip in and out. Can you blame us for thinking you did it?"

"It's not fair," Paul muttered.

"What's not fair?" Mr. Hartman asked.

"Nothing's fair," said Paul fiercely. "Everyone around here blames me for things I didn't do."

Mr. Hartman looked at him kindly. "Maybe there's a reason. Maybe you do get blamed for *some* things you don't do, but that's because of the things that you do do. I'm going to call your mother and ask her to come over."

Paul nodded gloomily.

When his mother arrived, Paul burst into tears. He didn't mean to, but he did.

His mother looked horrified when she heard what had happened. "No wonder you had a stomachache," she said, turning to Paul. Then she gasped. "I don't mean to say that he did this, Mr. Hartman. I can't imagine that he would do such a thing . . ."

"He complained of a stomachache?" Mr. Hartman sighed. "I'm afraid that does it. I suggest that he go home now and think about it overnight. Maybe tomorrow he will tell us about it."

"It's hard for me to believe that Paul would do anything as senseless as this. It's not like him . . ." His mother's voice trailed off. Paul looked at her hopefully, but she looked almost as helpless as he felt. "I know Paul has a temper," she said, "but he doesn't lie. He never has . . ."

Mr. Hartman looked from Paul to his mother. "I don't think Paul wants to lie. I think it's more that he's afraid to tell the truth. But maybe when he thinks it over, he'll change his mind. Maybe this time he just let his temper go too far."

Paul sat in his room the rest of the day wishing he had never been born. Or if he had to be born that bagels had never been invented. He wished his parents would move a million miles away from school, from Mrs. Dennis, from Mr. Hartman, and from all the kids. Especially from Dick Matthews.

When his father came home that evening, Paul didn't want any supper. "I don't feel like eating," he said. "Can't we move away from here?"

"No, we can't, Paul. Besides, that wouldn't solve anything," his father said.

"I didn't do it," Paul said.

"Supposing we say you didn't do it. Then who did? Someone did. In law you're innocent until you're proven guilty, but it doesn't always work that way. You've got yourself a bad

reputation, and now you're paying for it. Everyone thinks you did it, and now you've got to prove you didn't."

"How do I do that?" Paul demanded.

"I don't know. Find out who did, I suppose. Be a detective."

Paul liked that idea, but he didn't know how to go about it. He had nothing to go on but a lot of half-eaten bagels.

"I don't think you're lying, Paul, and neither does your mother. But this is a situation you're going to have to get out of yourself. We can swear up and down that you didn't do it, but if everyone else thinks you did, what we say isn't going to help you any. We're your parents, and everyone will say naturally we'd defend you. The only help we can give you is that we believe you."

"He's right," said Paul's mother, but she looked at him with troubled eyes. When she kissed him good-night she gave him an extra warm hug.

Paul sat in his room and stared out of his window at the school grounds. It was still light out and he had a clear view of the building. He sat and he thought and he thought. He had been in trouble before, but never anything as bad as this. He could see no end to it.

As he sat staring out of his window, he thought about what his father had said. He had to get out of this mess himself.

His father had said that if he didn't do it, someone else did. Who? Maybe that twerp Dick Matthews . . . it would be just like him to let Paul get blamed for it. But Paul had to give up on that thought. Dick lived way at the other end of town and he couldn't very well have asked his mother to drive him over to break into the school. Someone else had to have done it.

Paul got into his pajamas and stretched out on his back in his bed. Through his window he could see the moon shining brightly and there were even some stars. Then suddenly he had an idea, and he jumped out of bed. The school and the playground were as clear in the moonlight as they were in the daytime. If someone had broken into the school once, maybe they'd do it again. If he stayed up and watched at the window maybe he'd be able to see who it was. He wasn't very hopeful, but at least he'd be doing something.

Paul pulled up a chair next to the window and curled up in it. The school looked eerie in the moonlight and Paul was scared. What if some thief came sneaking into the school? What would he do? How could he stop him?

Paul's mind was filled with wild thoughts, and then all of a sudden he realized that his eyes were half-closed and he was almost asleep. He jumped up and crept out into the hall to the bathroom and doused his face with cold water. He ran back to his room so that he wouldn't miss anything.

He had to force himself to stay awake. He turned on his rock tumbler thinking the noise might do it, but the steady

whir only made him sleepier so he turned it off. Sometimes he thought he saw a shadow cross the lawn, but it turned out to be just the shadow of a tree wavering in the moonlight. He got very hungry and wished that he had made a sandwich for himself, but he didn't dare go down to the kitchen for fear of waking his parents.

Sometimes he was almost ready to give up and go to bed, and then he'd do some knee bends to wake himself up. He had never stayed up all night before and he hadn't realized how hard it was.

Paul sat in his chair concentrating on keeping his eyes open, when suddenly he saw three small figures running across the school grounds. One was a little larger than the other two. He wasn't sure what they were, but they certainly were animals. Paul leaned out the window. They were heading right for the school building. They acted as if they knew where they were going. Without any hesitation the big one went right to one of the small basement windows, and before Paul's very eyes, it gave the window a push inward, and scampered into the building with the two little ones following.

Paul was beside himself. He wished that he could fly out of his window right across the playground and into the school after the animals.

Instead, he tiptoed down the stairs softly in his bare feet and went out the front door, closing it gently behind him. Once outside, he ran across the lawn and across the school grounds and to the same basement window. He pushed the window open wider, and feet first, on his back, slid through the small opening. He looked around the basement but saw no sign of the animals. Then he heard a loud bang above him. It sounded as if a chair had been overturned.

He found the stairs and raced up them. He headed directly for the art room. Paul couldn't believe his eyes. Three raccoons were eating the remaining bagels as if they hadn't eaten in months. They looked so funny and were eating so methodically and seriously that Paul burst out laughing. They didn't seem to mind. They seemed friendly and tame. One of the little ones scurried away when he came near, but soon came back to the feast, and the other two went right on eating.

"So you're the ones." Paul stood away from them watching them devour the bagels, alternating between thinking the whole thing was a joke, and feeling stupid that he didn't know what to do.

Then his mind started working. Outside, in the school yard, there was a big wire basket for trash. That would make a perfect cage.

Paul opened one of the school doors from the inside and ran out and brought in the wire basket. If he ever got a raccoon into it, he would need a top to keep it closed. He looked all around for a suitable top but couldn't find anything. The next best thing would be to turn the basket upside down, once

the raccoon was inside, and fasten it somehow so the raccoon couldn't turn it over and get out.

The big problem was to get one of the raccoons inside the basket.

Paul tried to put the basket over one of them. But the raccoons thought it was a game, and soon the four of them were chasing one another all around the room. Paul became exhausted. He didn't think it was funny any more. Chairs were overturned, tables upset; the room looked as if it had been hit by a cyclone. Paul was frantic.

Finally one of the baby raccoons stopped to lick its paws. Paul immediately clapped the basket over the raccoon and pushed it into a corner. He then wedged the basket in with desks so that the basket couldn't move. All his activity frightened the other two, and they ran out of the room. A few minutes later, Paul saw them running across the lawn.

The room was a mess, but Paul didn't care. He made sure again that the basket was secure, and he walked out the school door. The moon was still bright in the sky, but Paul could see the sky growing light on the horizon. It would soon be daybreak. He crept back to his room and into bed, feeling too excited to ever fall asleep. But he closed his eyes and the next thing he knew, his mother was shaking him. "Paul, get up, get up. I've never seen you sleep so soundly."

Paul asked his mother to go to school with him that morning. "I'll go with you if you want," she said. "But, as Dad told you, what I have to say isn't going to count."

"You won't have to say anything. Just come."

Paul dressed quickly and ate his breakfast in a hurry. He wanted to get to school before his teacher and classmates arrived.

Paul and his mother waited in his classroom until the teacher and his class arrived. When everyone was there, Paul ran to get the principal, and asked them all to come into the art room.

"I hope you're not up to some trick," said Mrs. Dennis suspiciously.

"I want to show you something," said Paul.

Everyone looked mystified, but they followed him. At first all they saw was more crumbs and half-eaten bagels in the room. "I don't understand," said Mrs. Dennis.

Paul pointed to the corner. "Look in that cage. That guy did it. That one and his sister or brother and mother. They ate your bagels."

"A raccoon!" Mrs. Dennis shrieked. "How did it get in here? How do you know the raccoon did it?"

"I saw them do it," said Paul.

Paul explained how he had been determined to find out who had eaten the bagels and how he had stayed up all night to watch. He told them how he had seen the raccoons enter the

school, and the trouble it took to catch one. "And that's it. That's all."

His mother hugged and kissed him.

"I shouldn't have jumped to conclusions, Paul," said Mrs. Dennis. "I owe you an apology. I'm sorry."

"That's okay," said Paul.

After they cleaned up the room and let the raccoon go, Mrs. Dennis said, "The trouble is, we haven't got many bagels left to paint. Hardly any. And we used up our class money to buy them. We'll need something besides a few bagels and our pottery. Anyone have any ideas?"

No one did. George leaned over to Paul and said quietly, "If you brought in your polished rocks, I'd help you collect some more."

Paul thought about that for a few minutes. Yesterday, he'd hated school and everyone in it. Today, everything was still the same: the school, the kids, Mrs. Dennis, himself. Yet it was all different. There was a lot to try to figure out, but he felt good. "Yeah, I could do that," said Paul, and he did.